For my mother and father.
They did their best.
RA

To Hannah Butcher and her boys
PD

First US edition 2020

Library of Congress Catalog Card Number 2020921691
ISBN 978-1-5362-1266-2

21 22 23 24 25 CCP 10 9 8 7 6 5 4

Printed in Shenzhen, Guangdong, China

This book was typeset in Archer.
The illustrations were done in ink and paint and rendered digitally.

Candlewick Press
99 Dover Street
Somerville, Massachusetts 02144

www.candlewick.com

The American Society for Deaf Children endorses this book because it stresses the importance of full language and communication access for children and allows deaf children to see themselves represented in a story.

Can Bears Ski?

Raymond Antrobus

illustrated by
Polly Dunbar

CANDLEWICK PRESS

Dad Bear has a hard time waking me up in the morning.

"ONE."
The radiator shakes.

"TWO."
The bed rumbles like a large empty tummy.

"THREE."
The windows by the bed tremble.

"FOUR."
Dad Bear takes one heavy step forward.

The ceiling cracks.

"FIVE . . ."

My eyes snap awake.

I explode out of bed!

My feet hit the ground.

"I'M UP! I'M UP!"

I put on sky-blue socks

and my orange pants
and yellow sweater.

I like my colors
LOUD!

It's been snowing!

Everything feels still—
no rumbling,
no trembling.
It's like everything
is breathing quietly.

Then I feel Dad's voice.

"ONE."
Banisters shake.

"TWO."
Pictures wobble.

"THREE."
Stairs flinch.

"I'm coming. I'm coming!" I say.

I gobble-gobble breakfast.
Dad Bear has the TV on.
I can see a man in a blue snowsuit
skiing fast down a slope.

Dad Bear is saying something to me.

I think he says, **"Can bears ski?"**

I shrug.
I'm not sure I heard him right.

I eat the last of my porridge.
Time for school.

Dad Bear talks a lot on our way to school. I hear the crunch **crunch** **crunch** of the snow.

Dad Bear stops and looks directly at me. "Your friend was saying hello. Why did you ignore him?" "I didn't." *I didn't.*

Then Dad Bear asks again, **"CAN BEARS SKI?"**

Is that really what he's asking me?

Teacher Bear approaches Dad Bear.
I can only hear little pieces
of what they are saying.

"... have to sit ...

front of class ..."

Teacher Bear stamps on the ground.
I feel the ground shake, so I look up.

He is saying something to me,
but I can't quite work it out.
I wonder if it's **"Can bears ski?"**

David Bear sits next to me at lunch. He is talking a lot.
Suddenly laughter bursts out everywhere.
I don't know what everyone is laughing at.

He asks me a question.
"Can bears ski?"

I don't know.

Shhhhhhhh.

One day Dad Bear picks me up early.
We are going to meet someone
with a name I can't say.

She writes her name like this:
au-di-ol-o-gist.
It's a really hard word to say.

She puts headphones on my head.
She wants me to put a block on
the table every time I hear a sound.

Then she shows us something called an **au-dio-gram**.

It's also a hard word to say.

On the **au-dio-gram**, my results are the shape of a ski slope.

I imagine myself skiing down it.

The au-di-ol-o-gist asks,

"CAN BEARS SKI?"

After a week and
a few more
tests . . .

I start hearing therapy and
lip-reading classes, too!

The au-di-ol-o-gist gives me plastic ears called hearing aids.

They feel uncomfortable at first. Everything sounds like robots.

The au-di-ol-o-gist asks, "C

AN YOU
HEAR
ME?"

Whoa . . . Is life this loud?

Sometimes I get tired and sound stops making sense, no matter how loud it is.

Sometimes I take my hearing aids out and lose them. Guess I'm not used to them yet.

Can bears ski?

I still don't know
how to answer that question.

Dad Bear reads a story aloud.
He looks directly at me.
I can see his whole face,
and he speaks clearly.

I can feel his big voice and
see the words on the page,
so I follow Dad Bear's finger.

There is a big picture
of the moon.

I know what the moon is saying
because I can see its whole face,
and the moon is speaking clearly.

"Can you hear me?"
says the moon.

I say,

"Bears CAN ski!"